Finn

M

award

Finn's house was close to the sea. He could hear the sound of the waves from his bed.

But one night there was no noise at all. As Finn got up to look, a fairy flew into his room!

"Finn," she cried, "I need your help! The sea king sent me. The white horses have gone. When there are no white horses, there are no waves."

Finn was happy to help.

The fairy took his hand and they flew out of the window and over the sea.

"We must dive under the sea," she said.

"How long will I have to hold my breath?" asked Finn.

"Don't worry. My magic will help," said the fairy.

As soon as they were in the sea, the fairy turned into a mermaid!

Finn and the mermaid swam deep beneath the waves.

Finn saw lots of starfish on the sea bed. But there were no white horses.

As they swam on, they found a merman.

“I tried to catch the white horses in my net, but they were too quick,” said the merman.

Next, they saw a school of merchildren.

"Have you seen the white horses?" asked Finn.

"Yes. They swam by not long ago," said the merchildren.

Finn and the mermaid swam to the kelp forest.

"Look!" cried Finn. "There they are."

The white horses were eating the seaweed.

Finn spoke to the white horses.

"The sea is not the same without you. Please will you come back and make the waves?" he asked.

"Yes," they agreed. They were happy Finn had come to find them.

The mermaid took Finn to the sea king.

"You are so brave," said the sea king. "Thanks to you, the white horses will go back and make the waves."

It was time for Finn to go home.

He waved to the mermaid. “Goodbye!”

The mermaid waved back. “Thank you, Finn!” she cried.

A white horse took Finn back to the beach. The waves began to crash again.

Finn waved goodbye and went home. He soon fell asleep to the sound of the sea.

white horses

Where did Finn find the white horses?

mermaid

What other stories do you know with fairies or mermaids in them?

sea king

How would you describe the sea king.

Finn

How do you think
Finn felt when
he found the
white horses?

waves

Why are the waves
important to Finn?

starfish

How many starfish
did you see in
the story?

Notes for Parents and Teachers

Popular Rewards Early Readers have been specially created to build young readers' vocabulary, develop their comprehension skills and boost their progress towards independent reading.

★ Make reading fun. Why not read the story and have your child clap when they hear a featured phonics sound, then race to find it on the page?

★ Encourage your child to read aloud to help pick up and resolve any difficulties. As their skills grow, it will also help their fluency and expression.

★ The list of phonics sounds and 'tough and tricky' words will help to consolidate their learning.

★ Read and answer the questions together to develop comprehension and communication skills.

★ Always keep a positive attitude and focus on your child's achievements. This will help their confidence and build their enjoyment of reading.

ISBN 978-1-78270-598-7
Illustrated by Gary Rees

This edition first published 2023
Published by Award Publications Limited,
The Old Riding School, Welbeck, Worksop, S80 3LR
/awardpublications @award.books @award_books
www.awardpublications.co.uk
23-1055 1
Printed in China